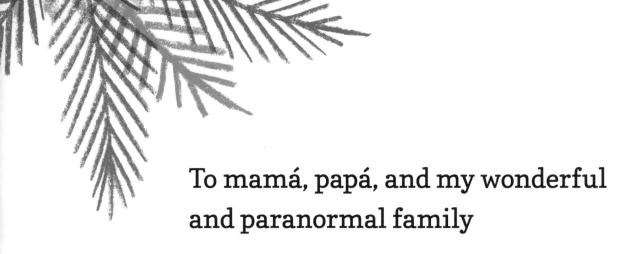

To mamá, papá, and my wonderful
and paranormal family

First U.S. edition 2020

Library of Congress Catalog Card Number pending
ISBN 978-1-5362-1114-6 (English hardcover)
ISBN 978-1-5362-1414-7 (Spanish hardcover)

LGO 25 24 23 22 21 20
10 9 8 7 6 5 4 3 2 1

Printed in Vicenza, Italy

This book was typeset in Copse.
The illustrations were done in mixed media.

Candlewick Press
99 Dover Street
Somerville, Massachusetts 02144

visit us at www.candlewick.com

CANDLEWICK PRESS

# GUSTAVO
## THE SHY GHOST

## FLAVIA Z. DRAGO

Gustavo was a ghost.

He enjoyed doing the normal things that paranormal beings do—passing through walls, making objects fly, and glowing in the dark.

But there was nothing in the world that he loved more than playing the violin.

Well . . . almost nothing.

Gustavo was secretly in love with Alma, the prettiest monster in town. But he also had a problem. . . .

You see, Gustavo was so shy that some things felt incredibly difficult for him.

And the worst part of it?

Making friends was terrifying.

Gustavo had never dared to speak
to any of the other monsters.

He tried getting
close to them

in many

different

ways.

But even when he was right in front of them . . .

they just couldn't see him.

Gustavo longed to be a part of something.

More than anything,
he wanted to make a friend.

I have to be brave.
I have to let the others see me!
he thought.

So, he decided to send a letter.
A very special one.

DEAR MONSTERS,
I would like to invite you
to my violin concert,

which will take place
at the Day of the Dead
party next full moon
at the cemetery.

I would be thrilled
to see you there.
GUSTAVO, THE GHOST

As the days went by, Gustavo
couldn't stop thinking . . .
What if no one shows up?
What if they don't
like my music?
What if they don't like me?

Except tonight was The Night.
And this time, he couldn't hide.

CHUTA

But not a soul had come.

So, all alone, Gustavo did what he loved most.

And the music made him happy.

So happy that he glowed.

Oh, how he glowed!

GUSTAVO!

From that moment on,
Gustavo's life changed.

And everyone
discovered that even
if he didn't talk much . . .

he was the best
at helping

and protecting
his friends.

But mostly, Gustavo never stopped surprising them.

And they never stopped loving him.